I Wish I Was Tall Like Willie
Quisiera ser tan alto como Willie

Written by / Escrito por Kathryn Heling and Deborah Hembrook

Illustrated by / Ilustrado por Bonnie Adamson

Translated by / Traducido por Eida de la Vega

For my brother Karl, short in stature but mighty!
— KEH
For Todd, love from your other mom.
— Aunt Debbie

For Mollie-dog.
— BCA

Heling, Kathryn and Hembrook, Deborah

I Wish I Was Tall Like Willie / written by Kathryn Heling and Deborah Hembrook ; illustrated by Bonnie Adamson; translated by Eida de la Vega = Quisiera ser tan alto como Willie / escrito por Kathryn Heling and Deborah Hembrook; ilustrado por Bonnie Adamson; traducción al español de Eida de la Vega — 1st ed. – Mc Henry, IL :Raven Tree Press, 2008.

     p. ; cm

Text in English and Spanish.

    Summary: Manuel goes to elaborate and comical lengths to be tall like his friend.
        He realizes that he has something that is just as desirable to be strong.
        Manuel gains appreciation of his own uniqueness.

ISBN: 978-0-9794462-0-7 Hardcover
ISBN: 978-0-9794462-1-4 Paperback

    1. Social Situations / Self Esteem & Self Reliance—Juvenile fiction. 2. Social Situations / Friendship—Juvenile fiction.
3. Boys and Men—Juvenile fiction. 4. Bilingual books—English and Spanish. 5. [Spanish language materials—books.]
I. Illust. Adamson, Bonnie. II. Title. III. Quisiera ser tan alto como Willie.

Library of Congress Control Number: 2007939497

Printed in Taiwan
10 9 8 7 6 5 4 3 2 1
First Edition

I Wish I Was Tall Like Willie
Quisiera ser tan alto como Willie

Written by / Escrito por Kathryn Heling and Deborah Hembrook

Illustrated by / Ilustrado por Bonnie Adamson

Translated by / Traducido por Eida de la Vega

Raven Tree Press

A Division of Delta Publishing Group

I wish I was tall like Willie.
He looks like a famous basketball player!

Quisiera ser tan alto como Willie.
¡Parece un famoso jugador de baloncesto!

Willie and I play outside.
I walk with stilts.
I love being tall!

Willie y yo jugamos afuera.
Me pongo zancos para caminar.
¡Me encanta ser alto!

I spiked my hair.
It stood straight up and I looked taller.

Me ericé el pelo.
Se quedó parado y así parecía más alto.

By recess, my hair was a gooey mess.
I'll never do THAT again!

A la hora del recreo, tenía el pelo hecho un desastre.
¡No lo volveré a hacer jamás!

I asked Dad to raise the seat on my bike.
I liked being taller.

Le pedí a mi papá que elevara el asiento de mi bicicleta.
Me gusta estar muy alto.

13

But then I couldn't reach the pedals.

Pero entonces no pude alcanzar a los pedales.

I tucked rolled up
socks in my shoes.

Metí los calcetines enrollados
dentro de los zapatos.

I stood two inches taller.

Parecía dos pulgadas más alto.

17

When I tried to walk, my shoes fell off.
I'll never do THAT again.

Cuando traté de caminar, los zapatos se me cayeron.
¡No lo volveré a hacer jamás!

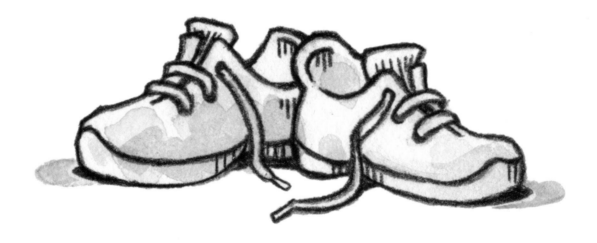

At the fair, I ran to the Fun House.

En la feria, entré en la Casa de los espejos.

I looked tall in the funny mirror.
But Willie laughed and laughed.

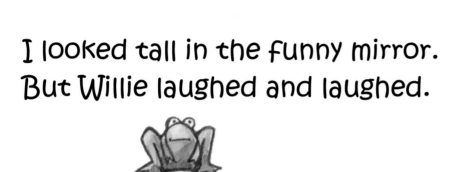

Al mirarme en el espejo, parecía alto.
Pero Willie se reía sin parar.

In the school play,
I really WAS the tallest kid on stage.

En la obra de teatro de la escuela,
yo ERA el niño más alto del escenario.

Then my hat got tangled in the curtain.
I never want to be tall like THAT again!

Entonces el sombrero se me enredó en la cortina.
¡NO quiero ser ASÍ de alto nunca más!

I still wish I was tall
like Willie.

Todavía quiero ser tan alto
como Willie.

But Willie wishes HE was strong like me!

¡Pero Willie quiere ser tan fuerte como yo!

29

Imagine that!

¡Imagínate!

Vocabulary
English

Vocabulario
Español

English	Español
tall	alto, alta
basketball	el baloncesto
hair	el pelo
Dad	el papá
seat	el asiento
bike	la bicicleta
socks	los calcetines
shoes	los zapatos
mirror	el espejo
school	la escuela